BOOK REVIEWS

Here's what people are saying:

*Jolly illustrations will open
the door to independent reading and
provide listening pleasure
for 4–5 year olds.*
from SCHOOL LIBRARY JOURNAL

OLIVER *is amusing in its account of
an elephant looking for a home.
Since children are such advocates of
the absurd, they'll enjoy Oliver's
trip through the city streets . . .
Easily readable.*
from THE NEW YORK TIMES

Weekly Reader Books presents

OLIVER

Story and pictures by SYD HOFF

An I CAN READ Book®

HARPER & ROW, PUBLISHERS, NEW YORK, EVANSTON, AND LONDON

OLIVER

Library of Congress catalog card number: 60-5779

OLIVER

Some elephants came across the ocean

on a ship.

They were going to work in the circus.

One elephant's name was Oliver.

When they landed

the circus man counted them:

"One, two, three, four, five,
six, seven, eight, nine, ten elephants."

"And one makes eleven," said Oliver.

"There must be a mistake.

I ordered only ten elephants,"

said the circus man.

"We don't need eleven."

11

"I won't take up much room,"
said Oliver.

"Elephants always do,"
said the circus man.

"Good-bye, Oliver,"

said the other elephants.

"Take good care of yourself."

Oliver was all alone.

He didn't know where to go.

little mouse came along.

Why don't you try the zoo?"

id the mouse.

You look like the type they use there."

Thanks, I'll go at once," said Oliver.

"Taxi!" said Oliver.

"What you need is a moving van,"
said the taxi man.

He did not stop.

16

Oliver followed the cars.

The drivers held out their hands

when they made a turn.

When Oliver made a turn

he held out his trunk.

He saw a woman weighing herself.

'My goodness,

'm as heavy as an elephant," she said.

Oliver got on the scale.

"I'm as heavy as an elephant, too,"
he said.

At last Oliver reached the zoo.

"Who is in charge here?" he asked.

"I am," said a man.

"Do you need an elephant?" asked Oliver.

"I'm sorry, not right now,"
said the zoo man.

"Thanks anyway," Oliver said
and walked away.

man was selling peanuts.

May I help you sell them?" asked Oliver.

Would you sell them or eat them?"

ked the man.

Eat them," said Oliver.

he man gave him some peanuts

r being honest.

Oliver left the zoo.

He walked down the street.

"Would anyone like to have me for a pe

he asked.

"I have a parakeet," said one person.

"I have goldfish," said another person.

"I have a cat," said another person.

"I have a duck," said someone else.

"I'd like a dog for a pet," said a lady.

"I can pretend I'm a dog," said Oliver.

"All right," she said.

Oliver and the lady went for a walk.

"Bowwow," said Oliver.

"What a nice dog," said the people.

"He's the biggest dog we ever saw!"

"I am hungry," said Oliver.

"Let's go home."

"Don't you have any hay?" he asked.

"No, but I have a nice bone,"

said the lady.

"Elephants need hay," Oliver said.

"I guess I can't be your dog after all.

But thank you, and good-bye."

"Good-bye," said the lady.

Oliver walked and walked.

Some people were riding horses.

Oliver watched.

"Horses get hay.

I wish I were a horse," he said.

"Do you need a horse?" asked Oliver.

"You look like an elephant.

But I'll ride you," said a man.

The man sat on Oliver's back.

"Giddyap," he said.

The horses jumped over the fence.

Plop!

Oliver could not jump over the fence.

"I guess I'm not a horse," he said.

"Good-bye."

"Good-bye," said the man.

Oliver passed a playground.

"May I play?" he asked.

"You may swing us," said the children.

"Is this the way?" asked Oliver.

"Not quite," said the children.

"But it will do."

"How does this work?" asked Oliver.

"It's a seesaw.

We'll get on the other side,"

said the children.

"Well?" asked Oliver.

The children rushed for the slide.

They couldn't all get on at once.

Oliver helped out.

It was time to rest.

The children talked about

what they wanted to be

when they grew up.

"I want to be a policeman," said Tomm

"I want to be a nurse," said Mary.

"I want to be a cowboy," said Ben.

"I always wanted to work in the circus,"
aid Oliver.

"I could be a dancing elephant."

He started to dance for the children.

Everybody stopped to watch.

They didn't see the circus parade coming.

They all watched Oliver.

They didn't see the acrobats.

They didn't see the jugglers.

They didn't see the clowns!

"Are they looking at me?"

asked the lion tamer.

"No," said the lion.

"They're looking at some elephant dancing."

"What's going on here?"

said the circus owner.

He ran over to look.

"That's the best dancing elephant
I've ever seen," he said.

"It's Oliver!" cried the other elephants.

"Oliver," said the circus man,

"I made a big mistake. We do need you.

Will you join the circus?"

"I'd love to," said Oliver.

"Hurray," cried the children.

"You got your wish!"

"Will you remember us?"

asked the children.

"Of course," said Oliver.

"An elephant never forgets."

"And even a rhinoceros

would remember the fun we had."